The Best Bit of
Daddy's
Day

For Dennis, the best daddy I know!
C.A.

MIX
Paper
FSC FSC® C018306

First published in Great Britain 2016
by Egmont UK Limited,
The Yellow Building, 1 Nicholas Road, London W11 4AN
www.egmont.co.uk

Text and illustrations copyright © Claire Alexander 2016

Claire Alexander has asserted her moral rights.

ISBN 978 1 4052 7645 0

A CIP catalogue record for this title is available from the British Library.

The Best Bit of
Daddy's
Day

Claire Alexander

EGMONT

My name is Bertie and my daddy
is a builder. He drives diggers
and trucks every day!

Today he's going to go up in his
crane and build a tall tower.
When I'm big I want to be
a builder just like him . . .

. . . but I'm only little,
so I go to school.

Daddy drops me off on his
way to work. "Have a good
day, Bertie!" he says.

When the bell goes

BRRRIIING

I run into class.

"Good morning, everyone," says my teacher.
"Today we're going to be builders."

This is going to be a brilliant day!

First she reads us an exciting story about a digger.

Then I paint a picture of
a crane like Daddy's.
But someone spoils it . . .

and at lunchtime I trip over.

I feel sad. I wish I could see my daddy.

So I run to the playground
and go up, up, UP . . .

. . . to the top of the climbing frame. I'm so high up I can see the top of Daddy's tower!

There's someone inside
the crane – it must be him!

In the afternoon we all build an enormous tower.

I'm the small crane, and we let our teacher

be the big crane because she's wearing

the highest shoes.

Our tower is brilliant!

At home time Daddy picks me up and gives me his hat to keep my ears dry. I tell him that I was a builder today, and the best bit was making a tower, just like him.

Then I tell him about the not-so-good bits of my day – my spoiled painting and tripping over.

"I bet things like that never happen to you, Daddy," I say.

"Well, actually," says Daddy . . .

"... they do sometimes!

Today someone spoiled
my brand new floor,

and I tripped over at lunchtime, just like you!

But then I finished
my tower, and I think
I saw you, Bertie,
on the climbing frame!"

"It WAS me, Daddy!" I say, and I ask him if the best bit of his day was finishing the tower.

"The best bit of my day is right now," says Daddy, "being here with you, Bertie."

I snuggle up and say,
"Well actually, Daddy, I think this
is the best bit of my day, too."

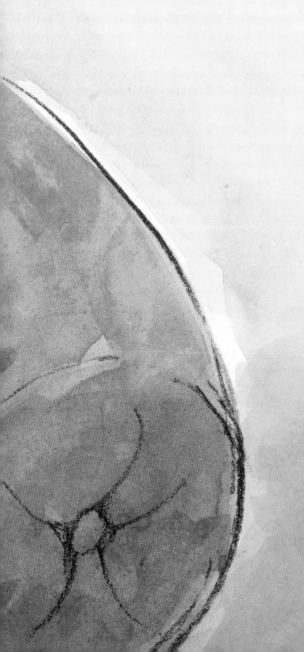

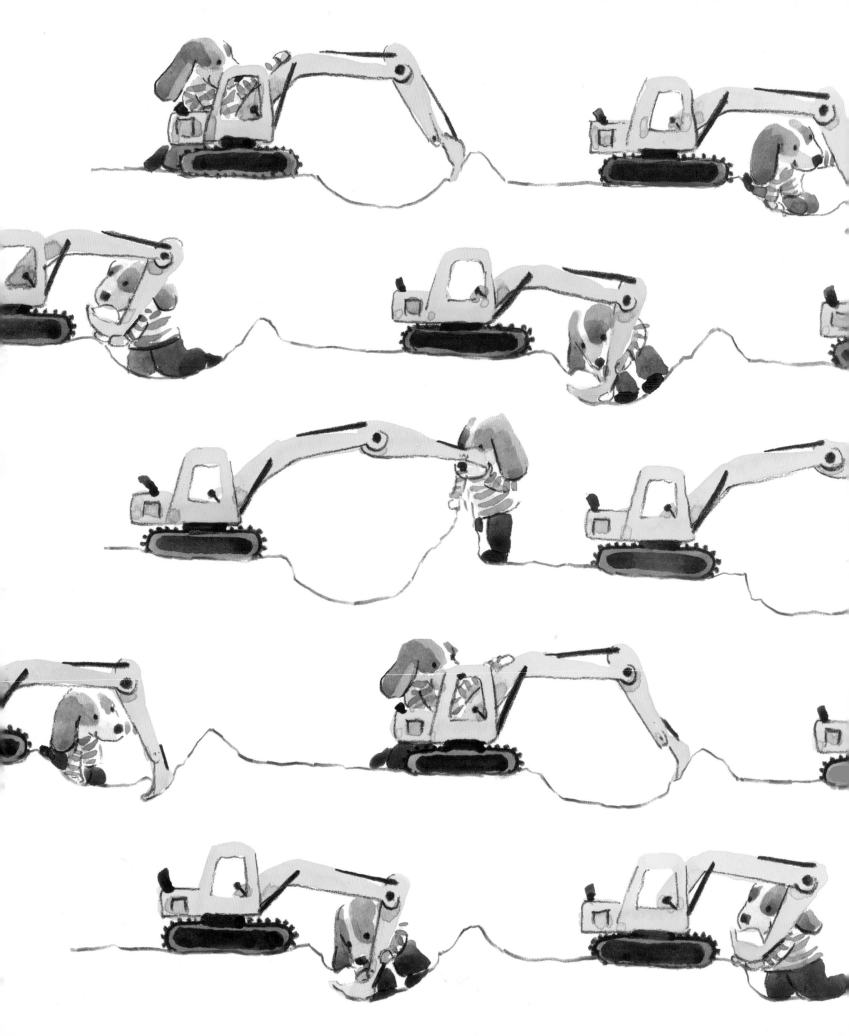